A CENTURY
OF STORIES
NEW HANOVER COUNTY PUBLIC LIBRARY
1906-2006

Black and White Rabbit's ABC

Alan Baker

BOSTON

KINGFISHER
a Houghton Mifflin Company imprint
222 Berkeley Street
Boston, Massachusetts 02116
www.houghtonmifflinbooks.com

First published in hardcover in 1994
First published in paperback in 1995
This paperback edition published in 1999
4 6 8 10 9 7 5 (HC)
8 10 9 7 (PB)
7TR/0804/TWP/PW/150SEM

LIBRARY OF CONGRESS CATALOGING-IN-PUBLICATION DATA
Baker, Alan.
Black and White Rabbit's ABC/Alan Baker.—1st American ed.
p. cm.— (Little rabbit books)
Summary: The story of a rabbit's exhausting efforts to
paint a picture presents the letters of the alphabet.
[1. Alphabet. 2. Painting—Fiction. 3. Rabbits—Fiction.]
I. Title. II. Series: Baker, Alan. Little rabbit books.
PZ7.B1688B1 1994
[E]—dc20 93-29760 CIP AC

ISBN 1-85697-951-2 (HC)
ISBN 0-7534-5253-7 (PB)

Printed in Singapore

Aa

A is for apple.

Bb

B is for box,
where Rabbit
puts the apple.

Cc

C is for crayon,
held in Rabbit's paw.

Dd

D is for drawing.

Ee

E is for easel,
to rest Rabbit's
drawing on.

Ff

F is for falling
as the apple
topples over.

Gg

G is for glue,
icky-sticky
glue.

Hh

H is for hopping,
with a sticky paw.

Ii

I is for ink bottle,
right in Rabbit's way.

Jj

J is for jumping,
but not high enough!

Kk

K is for
kicking
it over.
Whoops!

Ll

L is for leaking
all over the floor.

Mm

M is the mess,
soon mopped up.

Nn

N is for nose,
covered in ink.

Oo

O is for
opening
a new jar
of paint.

Pp

P is for the paint,

a bright apple green.

Qq
Q is for quick! Paint in the picture.

Rr

R is for
runny,
the
paint's
not
thick
enough.

Ss

S is for
spilling
as paint
drips
off the
brush.

Tt

T is for
turning.

Uu

U is for
upside down.

Vv

V is for very good.
Rabbit's painting
is done.

Ww

W is for water
to wash
the brushes.

Xx

X is for the kisses that Rabbit draws on his painting.

Yy

Y is for yawning. What a hard day's work!

Zz

Z is for zzzzzzzzz.
Rabbit's fast asleep.